At Grandpa's Sugar Bush

To Fred and Pearl Barry and all their progeny
and to the Barry sugar bush in Haliburton County,
Ontario — the most beautiful place in the world
to welcome spring. — M.C.
With love to our grandpa and grandma,
Cory and Bea Wilson. — J.W.

First U.S. edition 1998

Text copyright ©1997 by Margaret Carney
Illustrations copyright © 1997 by Janet Wilson

Kids Can Press Ltd. acknowledges with appreciation the assistance of the Canada Council and
the Ontario Arts Council in the production of this book.

Published in Canada by
Kids Can Press Ltd.
29 Birch Avenue
Toronto, ON M4V1E2

Published in U.S. by
Kids Can Press Ltd.
85 River Rock Drive, Suite 202
Buffalo, NY 14207

The artwork in this book was rendered in oil on Masonite board.
Text set in Perpetua.

Edited by Debbie Rogosin
Printed in Hong Kong by Wing King Tong Company Limited

CMC 97 0 9 8 7 6 5 4 3 2

Canadian Cataloguing in Publication Data
Carney, Margaret (Margaret Rose)
At Grandpa's sugar bush

ISBN 1-55074-341-4

1. Sugar maple - Tapping - Juvenile literature. 2. Maple syrup - Juvenile literature. I. Wilson,
Janet, 1952- . II. Title.

SB239.M3C37 1997   j633.6'45   C96-931694-1

At Grandpa's Sugar Bush

Written by Margaret Carney

Illustrated by Janet Wilson

Kids Can Press

During spring school break I go to my grandpa's farm. He's working in the sugar bush and needs my help.

Warm weather in February made a hard crust on
the deep snow. We haul sap buckets and spiles to the
sugar bush on sleds.

In the fresh snow that fell overnight we see fox
tracks and weasel tracks. Red squirrels scold us from
the spruce trees on our way into the bush.

A flock of evening grosbeaks flies over. Grandpa says the funny *yank-yank* we hear is made by white-breasted nuthatches getting ready to nest in a crack in a big old maple tree.

We find the holes the pileated woodpeckers are making, and we often hear them drumming.

Many of the sugar maples are more than a hundred years old. Grandpa knows every tree in the bush, just as his dad did. Someday I will, too.

Grandpa drills a hole in the first maple tree, on the southeast side. The bright spring sun warms that side first. I clean out the wood shavings with a twig.

We put in a spile and tap it gently with a hammer. It seems to take forever, but finally a big drop of sap forms at the tip of the spile. I catch it on my tongue and taste its sweetness.

We hang a sap bucket from the spile and cover it
with a lid. For a while we can hear the *plink*, *plink* of
sap dripping onto the bottom of the bucket.

Grandpa says the first robin always sings on the day
the sap starts to run.

After lunch the sun grows warm
and the snow becomes soft. Grandpa's
feet leave deep holes in the snow.
Mine leave little holes. Snowfleas
gather in our footprints. They're
another sign of spring, Grandpa says.

Every day we collect the sap,
carrying it to big barrels near the
boiling place. Last October Grandpa
felled dead trees, then cut and split
them into firewood. I helped him
haul and pile it.

Grandpa digs snow out of the boiling place and I bring him the pieces of stovepipe. When everything is ready and the sap barrels are full, we start the fire. First smoke, then heat waves rise up the chimney.

Soon steam from the sap pan will smell sweet and mapley. Whenever we're thirsty we cool boiling sap in the snow and drink it. It gets sweeter and sweeter — and stickier.

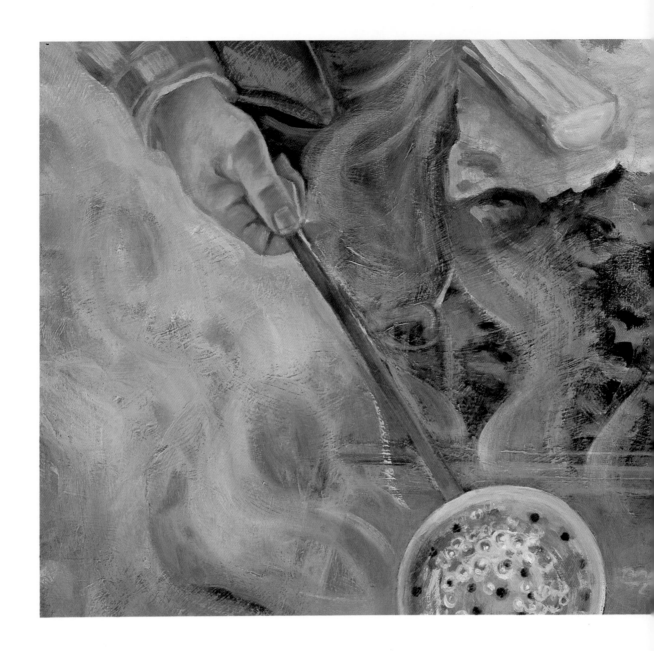

We keep adding sap to the boiling pan — if it boils dry the syrup will burn. Grandpa skims off the foam with a large tin spoon full of holes. Every hour he builds up the fire in the long tunnel under the sap pan.

I ask him to let me put the first stick on the bed of
glowing red coals. The heat makes my face tingle.

Grandpa goes back to the sugar bush after supper, but I go to bed. Working in the bush makes you hungry and very tired.

One night he lets me come along. A big sugar moon lights our path.

Finally the syrup is ready. It drips from the ladle in a sheet. Grandpa carefully draws the sap pan off the fire onto green poles we propped up on forked sticks.

I help him strain the syrup through a cloth to remove bits of dirt and ash. Then we get to clean the pan. We scrape the thick, sticky syrup from the bottom with wooden spoons Grandpa carved out of cedar. It's yummy!

We pour the warm syrup into old cream cans. When it's cool, we haul the cans out of the bush on the sled, back to the farmhouse.

The next morning we have maple syrup and pancakes for breakfast. Grandma says Grandpa and I make the tastiest syrup in the county.

I think it's the best in the whole world.